What Happens in

Key West…

A Brody Wahl Novelette

Wayne Gales

To Captain Bob Moran
The Real Deal
Rest In Peace
See You On The Other Side
Hopefully Not Too Soon

Remembering our friend,
neighbor and fellow author
Malcolm Massey
You fought the good fight
We will miss you

"Everybody knows we're all gonna die, but ain't nobody knows when or why.

Some folks think they'll come back as a snake or a frog,
But me I'm comin back as a Schooner Wharf bar dog."
                                    Mike McCloud

Say hello to my good friend, Jake. Jake's not my dog, or a bar-dog, but the roommate of our good friend, MJ. Jake's been a houseguest when MJ took a Mexico Vacation.

He's part of this book, and I have portrayed him as accurately as possible, with the normal fiction book embellishments.

Welcome to the mystery writer's world, Jake.

You're a good fit.

Forward

Well, it took me a year to come up with some sort of plot, but here's book number twelve. I've been busy, working part-time at the golf course, producing a memoir for my good friend and amazing editor Peter Leonard, and producing a couple of children's books for my granddaughter, Ariel Torres. Add a couple of frame designs, some gardening, and a little travel with my best friend, soulmate, and wife, Tina, and I can honestly say the grass ain't growin' under my feet.

I keep saying, "This is my last book," but it's like a drug habit. As long as you can think of something to write, you write. I keep thinking about a different storyline, but after nearly fifteen years, I have decided I am the proverbial one-trick pony. My love of the Keys, and the fortunate, (or unfortunate, depending on how you look at it) association with some of Key West's true legends like Mel Fisher, Capt. Tony Terracino, Pat Clyne, Bob Moran, and later on Carl Fismer, along with people like Bill Black, Mel's daughter Taffi Fisher Abt, and Sherri Culpepper, who used to work for Mel and currently runs Key West Treasure Chest, and my path was set in stone. It didn't hurt that I had family ties that went back a dozen generations in the Keys and Bahamas, which prompted me to search history and ancestry.

Let's just say it's about all I know. Too late in life to start a career as a skydiver, bungee jumper, or underwear model.

If there's such a thing as guilt by association, then call me guilty. Is this it?

As I always say, "Never say never".

Stay tuned.

One

There's a danger with having too much money in the bank. You get lazy, or stupid. Oh, it's not like I'm rich, but with a little luck and some shrewd investing, my father left me with a comfortable bank account. Along the way, this time with more luck than brains, I have added a few dollars here and there. The result? Even living in one of the most expensive towns in America, good ol' Key West, the Conch Republic, The Rock, Cayo Hueso, whatever you want to call it, I don't have to work another day in my life. So what to do? Sit on a barstool at *Hunks* drinking mojitos with my friend and part-time bodyguard, Caretaker, until I grow old, fat, and ugly (I'm already two out of three), fall off that stool drunk and dead, and be swept aside like last night's plastic drink cup?

I don't think so. My wanderlust, or at least my lust and my liver, make that an unlikely scenario.

Like my father, I've had terrible luck with women. They either leave me, live too far away, steal from me, or worse yet, try to kill me.

I guess I could move to Israel, and at least be near my kids. I don't think Mallory would be interested in rekindling the relationship.

I think that ship has sailed.

Or, head back to Texas? As much as the lovemaking with Betty Jo was inventive and enthusiastic, A life clouded with nightly Fireball excursions would get old in a hurry.

Besides, I need regular doses of vitamin "O".

Ocean.

And I don't sleep alone anymore.

There's Jake.

What Happens in Key West…

Wayne Gales

2

Key West has no shortage of bar dogs. Some are strays that live on the streets, and some are residents' pets who sneak away from home during the day, hanging around the many outdoor establishments, mooching French fries, or scarfing up the occasional dropped fish stick or runaway shrimp. Wait staff and managers are tolerant of their furry patrons as long as they are not aggressive, and I've seen many a server sneak a treat to them after cleaning off a table. They know where they are welcome and where they are not.

One dog, a big labradoodle, was a regular around Schooner Wharf, B.O.'s Fishwagon, and the Conch Republic Seafood bar. He knew I was a soft touch for a handout, and I've been greeted more than once with a wet muzzle on a bare leg. He was clean, collared, and undoubtedly someone's pet. With a wire-hair coat that brought to mind the loopy side of Velcro tape, had he been a feral stray, his coat would have been a matted mess. The name on his collar said Jake, and he recognized his name. You need to greet a dog with something more than "Hey, dog". He seemed to warm to the name.

One afternoon after beer and oysters at *Schooner Wharf*, the skies darkened, and it looked like an afternoon thunderstorm was on the way. I paid my tab and walked to the Jeep. When I got there, Jake was sitting in the right seat like he belonged. He looked dirtier than normal with muddy feet and a matted coat. I wondered if his home situation had changed. I opened the passenger door. "Get out, Jake!" I pointed at the

5

ground. "This isn't your car!" He completely ignored me, staring straight forward like a statue. I took him by the collar, and he pulled back, determined. After a minute of coaxing, I looked at the darkening skies, heard the rumble of thunder, and said, "Okay, you can come home, but just until this rain stops, then, back you go." I swear he wiggled with pleasure like he understood every word.

When we got to Houseboat Row, Jake jumped out of the jeep over the door and, wagging his tail, waited impatiently for me to show him his new home. We walked inside, and Jake did a quick self-tour, selected a spot by the sliding glass door, and plopped down, feigning deep sleep in thirty seconds. "Don't get too comfortable," I warned him. "After the sun comes out, you're going back to Old Town."

He closed his eyes even tighter.

After a few minutes, a smelly dog odor began to engulf the room. It became unbearable in thirty. "You're not staying here for another second smelling the place up," I scolded Jake. He looked up at me as if he knew what I was saying. "You're going to get a bath."

At the word "bath", Jake got up, wagged his tail, and obediently trotted toward the bathroom. I think that dog had a better grasp of the English language than most humans.

Maybe more.

I undressed, and we showered together, using my human body wash for shampoo. After toweling him off, Jake got the zoomies for a few minutes before finding the only throw rug in the house, rolling violently until dry to his satisfaction. I smiled, shook my head, and made a couple of signs on blank paper. "Found dog.

Large, white wire-haired crossbreed," and my number. I also placed a *found* ad in the Key West Citizen.

We got in the Jeep and I posted the signs around *Schooner Wharf* and in front of B.O.'s *Fish Wagon*. In the meantime, I made a quick stop at the Winn Dixie for food. He could eat out of my elegant two-dollar Corel plastic dishes until he went back home. Until then, I guess I had a house guest until I got that call.

That call never came. After two weeks, I figured I now had a dog.

Or should I say, a dog had *me*.

Dogs have masters. Jake had *staff.* I'm thoroughly convinced Jake now owned a houseboat, a Jeep, and a boat, along with a full-time chauffeur to motor him around.

After all, you don't see him picking up *my* poop in a plastic bag do you?

Forget about a doggie bed. He had a king bed with a tropical-themed duvet that he grudgingly shared with yours truly every night. Oh, I didn't mind the companionship. I finally had someone to talk to who didn't talk back. Jake always carefully listened to my chatter and pondered every comment as if he were going to pass judgment. I used to talk to myself. Now I have someone to talk to, much like Tom Hanks talked to Wilson in Castaway, with about the same amount of response.

I never knew I needed a dog in my life until I had one.

It felt as natural as a warm bed or a favorite pair of sneakers.

It's not like I just sit around, consume alcohol at *Hunks*, and pet Jake at night. I go offshore fishing regularly, go spearfishing with buddies when the opportunity arises, and occasionally join one of many treasure boats in Key West and help look for that next ancient galleon, loaded with gold, silver, emeralds, and fabulous fame. Crews always welcome a diver with good gear, a sharp eye, and a reputation for being lucky. You dive for a share of the treasure, should there be any found, which means you usually work for no more than a baloney sandwich at lunch and a few semi-cool Bud Lights at day's end.

As they say, I'd rather be lucky than good.

Then there's my cohort in crime, Caretaker. He bailed on the *Hunk's* bouncer job in two months. He was about to go batshit crazy breaking up the rare bar fight or having to escort an inebriated customer off the property at two in the morning by his little pinkie.

Too dull for a soul that has been around that much.

To avoid dying of boredom, Caretaker started a private investigation business in Key West, hunting down deadbeat dads, cheating wives, loan skippers, and chasing down dine and dashers. Needless to say, on this Rock, it's a target-rich environment. I don't know if that line of business is exciting enough to melt his butter, but it sure keeps him busy and gives him the occasional opportunity to crack a few heads together, a perk that Caretaker finds enjoyable.

And just like that, I have a job now. Look at me, Brodrick Russell Wahl, Assistant Private Eye. Caretaker says he has more clientele than one man can handle, and I got recruited to pick up the overflow. I don't think he was that busy, but Caretaker, gruff old man that he is, needs an assistant, like Batman needs Robin, the Lone Ranger needs Tonto, or the Green Lantern needs Kato.

And a head needs lice.

Caretaker's more than twice as old as I am, but the friendship clicks. He's been around the horn, over the top, and down every alley on this planet. I don't know his history, but I suspect Caretaker and my father could have swapped some seriously tall tales and shared a few broken bone stories, both theirs and their opponents.

Compared to him, I've been barely around the block. Honestly, I don't think he would be happy if he didn't have someone or something to watch over.

First things first. After getting all the licenses and permits, we needed an office. Officially using his condo as a business address, we set up shop in a more comfortable spot – namely the two barstools closest to the street at *Hunks*, a location craftily designed to keep the rotation of the earth from making the bar top, the bar, and the entire island from flying off into space. From our "office," we could people-watch, shoot the breeze, wait for a phone call from some damsel in distress, and get on the outside of the occasional distilled grain beverage.

Hey, alcohol is a food group too, sort of.

Slow to start, we started picking up a few clients, mostly the junk mentioned above, things that were too insignificant to interest the local police, or matters that were *too* interesting to the police.

Either way, we were swimming in the shallow end of the gene pool.

Then Jane called.

Wayne Gales

3

"My husband is gone for days at a time, two or three times a month." Jane started, "I think he's seeing someone else."

"Cut and dried," Caretaker said after getting Jane's information. "We just tail the jerk for a few days, find out who the new tootsie is, give the info to the wife, and let her handle it from there. A quick one or two grand." Holding up his glass, he added, "At least it will cover the bar bill for a few weeks."

Neither of us really needed to work. Caretaker had some sort of retirement pension that he only vaguely mentioned. His quick meeting with Dad's old girlfriend back at his goodbye party made me suspect it was something government-related, but I was too polite to ask, and probably wouldn't have gotten a straight answer anyway.

Caretaker had arranged for Jane to meet us at Bayview Park. A bar on Duval Street might be just dandy for chasing a dine-and-dash crook, but maybe not that appropriate for a proper business visit with a proper lady.

Boy, did we get that part right.

Sitting on a bench at the park, a woman approached Caretaker, Jake, and me at the scheduled meeting time. She looked like a typical Key West local in typical Key

West attire, an outfit Dad used to call "Key West Camouflage," a loose knee-length shift with spaghetti straps.

Swimming around in a size-four dress, I would hazard she couldn't weigh more than eighty-five pounds soaking wet. She was hatless, no sunglasses, and worn Birkenstock sandals. No lipstick, no noticeable makeup, and her fingers and toes were unpainted. Her wispy blonde hair in a pixie cut that would look cute on an eight-year-old, but made Jane look small and frail. She was about the plainest person I'd ever seen. If I were a guessing man, had she not said the 'husband' word, I would have judged Jane was a woman of the lesbian persuasion, but as they say, "judge not lest ye be judged."

I saw that in a book somewhere.

Plain Jane. Well, so much for some hot, jilted bride, anxious to get even with a cheating husband. We stood and shook hands all around. She had a man's handshake and made me think "Army veteran", and, despite the initial impression, her hair looked clean and her dress neatly pressed. She had an amazing smile and the prettiest almond-colored eyes I've ever seen, all packaged in a plain brown wrapper.

Dad was always a sucker for eyes. He said they were a mirror to the soul.

Caretaker asked, "What makes you think he's seeing someone else?"

"He leaves for days at a time, two or three times a month," Jane started. "He says he's out fishing with his buddies, but he never brings home any fish. He doesn't even *smell* like fish." Looking at us with an inquiring face, she added, "Don't they use bait?"

Looking at me as the resident expert, Caretaker nodded for me to answer. "I go fishing with friends often." I replied, "And it ain't like they just come up and jump in your boat." I continued, "If he's gone fishing for days at a time, I would guess he's swordfishing. It's a great fish to put in a boat, but you can fish for days or weeks without luck. It's not surprising that he comes home empty-handed more often than not. That being said," I added, "You *do* use bait, usually mackerel, so no fishy smell *is* a little suspicious."

Caretaker cut to the chase. "Two hundred bucks a day," he growled, mostly, to see if she would put her money where her mouth was. "We'll tail him for a few nights. It shouldn't take that long to see if he's up to something fishy, so to speak."

Jane reached into her purse and handed over a wad of Ben Franklins. "Here's six days' worth. Will that be enough?"

"Enough for a start", Caretaker nodded, pocketing the cash without counting. "It could take just one night, or it could take a week or two." I was sure this mystery could be solved in a day, but Caretaker wanted to see just how serious she was. Jane gulped but nodded. "I have more if you need it." Standing up, she turned to walk away, then stopped. "One more thing," she added. "Jimmie has a record, and he hangs around some bad people. If you catch him, it could be dangerous for you, and maybe for me. Please be careful."

"I don't faint easy like," Caretaker answered slowly. Nodding toward me, he added, "We can take care of ourselves. I doubt Jimmie can throw anything our way we can't handle."

13

"As for you," I chimed in, "We'll make sure you're safe."

Caretaker looked toward me with furrowed eyes that said, *'Keep your dick in your pants, Brody.'*

'I know, I know," my eyes answered back. "I'm just protecting our client".

"Before you go," Caretaker asked, "What's his last name and what boat does he go out on?"

She answered, "Jones, the same as mine," She thought for a second, then answered his second question. "I think the boat is called *Slack Tide*."

"Can we walk you to your car?" I offered.

"Oh no, I don't drive," she answered, a little self-conscious. "I'm totally against exhaust pollution. My bike is parked on the rack by the tennis courts. I'm fine."

While we walked back to the Jeep, Caretaker chuckled. "Jim Jones." Was all he said.

"Is that significant?" I asked.

"Not really," he said with a little smile. "Just don't drink the Kool-Aid."

"Hunh?" I asked, puzzled.

"Never mind."

What Happens in Key West…

Wayne Gales

4

"Do you ever think with the big head?", Caretaker asked on the way to the Jeep. "That was about the homeliest human to walk the planet. As ugly as your mug is, I still think you can do a little better than that. Come to think of it," he mused, rubbing his beard, "I've seen you do worse."

"Think of it this way," I answered, a little indignantly. "Jane's a cash-paying customer, and it's not like that level of clientele is exactly piling up on your doorstep, er, in front of your barstool...until we know the story, we need to protect our commodity."

"Just try to stay on the daylight side of that *commodities'* dress," Caretaker counseled.

Uncomfortable with that line of schooling (*it's like he has a microscope in my brain*), I changed the subject. "So, Mr. Private Eye Boss, where do we start?"

Holding up one finger, Caretaker started counting. "First, we find the boat, then scout it out for a couple of nights to see if our friend is actually going fishing. Your damsel in distress didn't even tell us where *Slack Tide* is berthed."

"I know people," I answered confidently. "A few calls and I can locate the boat. I'm sure it's either at Garrison Bight or someplace on Stock Island."

After a few calls, I found the slip at Garrison Bight where slack tide was tied up, just a few dozen spots away from where my boat, *Whisper*, was berthed. We drove by and I saw the tail art. I smiled with satisfaction as I saw the *Rodeo* was parked two slips down. I knew Captain Randy. I'd give him a call and get the ok to sit in the flying bridge for a few nights so I could watch slack tide come in. At least we would know if Jimmie was *really* going fishing.

We drove by *Slack Tide* every night for a few days. On the third day, the slip was empty. "Well, if our friend Jimmy is cheating on his bride, he's doing it in the water," I noted. "Drop me off at the houseboat, and I'll walk over and wait in the *Rodeo* for her to come back and see if they scored."

For those of you mainlanders, unless you come to the Rock to fish, you have driven by Garrison Bight a dozen times without knowing it was called Garrison Bight. When you turn off Roosevelt onto Palm Avenue on the way to downtown, you cross a strip of land and a bridge with fishing charter boats on one side and houseboats on the other. That's Garrison Bight, and where I live.

I only had to walk across the street, playing a game of 'Key West Frogger' during midday traffic times, but easy-peasy in the middle of the night. I found my friend's boat and climbed up onto the bridge.

It took me a whole three hours to decide that this private-eye shit is boring. *Really* boring, and it was three nights before our guest of honor showed back up. The seat on *Rodeo's* bridge isn't designed for extensive sitting and my ass got numb in a few hours. After the first night, I climbed down and nestled in the fighting chair. I could see two slips over just as easily as I could while perched fifteen feet in the sky.

Around three-thirty in the morning on day three, I heard the rumble of twin diesels and watched *Slack Tide* pull into her slip. In the dim light, I saw three figures tie up the boat and walk down the dock in my direction with nothing more than a couple of backpacks. I quickly spun the fighting chair around in case they saw me.

"Well, that was underwhelming," I muttered to myself. After seeing them drive away in three different cars, I climbed out of *Rodeo* and went home to bed.

"Whadaya think?", Caretaker asked the next morning over coffee and a croissant.

"I just saw three fishermen come back from a few days of no-luck fishing," I answered, trying to copy Caretaker's dry humor. "That's why they call it *fishing,* not *catching.*"

"Well, that's that," Caretaker said, conclusively, finishing up his coffee and standing up. "We let her know hubby's not a cheater, give her the rest of her money back, and try to solve some old lady's missing parakeet mystery."

"Not so fast", I cautioned. "I think there might be a little more to the story, and for some reason, and I doubt she will be satisfied with, 'He's a good boy, now go back to your National Enquirer.' Oh, I don't mind giving her the rest of her money back, but I have a couple of ideas to follow up on."

"Yeah, I bet you have a few 'ideas'", Caretaker answered, still standing up. "If you're gonna chase tail, perhaps you should stick to a more, ah, target-rich, environment, like Duval Street after two a.m."

I tried to look hurt. "Look, Mr. Falkenburg, she's a nice lady, and I don't think she'll be satisfied, with 'he's faithful, suck it up, buttercup'."

Caretaker growled dangerously. "I told you to never call me by that name again." But I could tell I hit a tender button. "Okay, Brody, you can do a little more sleuthing, but don't ask me to come hold your hand."

Wayne Gales

5

Jane and I met for coffee at Two Friends Patio on Caroline a few days later. Like before, she was wearing a plain, print dress that went down to her ankles, no makeup, and Birkenstock shoes. She either has a dozen copies of the same dress, or she takes it off every night, washes, and dries it. If Jane got any plainer, she would vanish into the walls. As I expected, Plain Jane was not satisfied with the "he's just going fishing" answer.

"Why does he go fishing for three days at a time and never catch anything?" Jane asked. "As I said, I don't even *smell* fish when he gets home."

"Maybe he's just a bad fisherman," I countered, handing her a wad of bills, refunding the balance of her fee. Jane pushed the money back into my hands.

Her touch was gentle and her hands were soft.

(*Down, boy*)

"Can't you find out what he's really doing?" she implored. "I'll pay you this and enough for another week. I think Jimmy and his hoodlum friends are up to no good."

Caretaker and I met at *Hunks* that afternoon. After listening to her concerns and the promise of further pay, he quizzed.

"So, Oh Mr. Super Sleuth, what's your next brilliant step?"

"Actually, I have a couple of ideas," I answered smugly. "Let's just say a little apparel disguise. I wanna see if I can make him flinch a little."

Caretaker opened his mouth to say something, then shut it. He knew, like my dad, that if he asked, he probably wouldn't get a straight answer, and he *definitely* wouldn't change my mind.

Jane and I met for coffee every few days, sometimes at Two Friends, sometimes at *Pepe's*, and even occasionally at *Blue Heaven*. Never breakfast, just coffee, and never in the afternoon at *Hunks*. I suspect she either wasn't a drinker or dared not be seen in a den of inequity like *Hunks* around low-lifers like Caretaker and me. The Conversation was pleasant, if not a little shallow. After meeting three times, I knew about as much about Jane as I did about the tooth fairy.

It was almost two weeks before Plain Jane called and let us know Jimmy was gone again. I called Caretaker, and went over my plan with him.

My "apparel disguise" was hanging in my closet. During my short stint with Fish and Wildlife when I was hired to count sharks but instead ended up counting human body parts, I was issued a uniform. Well, actually just a couple of FWC shirts and baseball caps. I figured a late-night visit when slack tide pulled in would give me a chance to read body language. All I really wanted to know was if he was really a fisherman or just a *bad* fisherman. I knew it might mean another late night in an uncomfortable chair, but hey, I've closed *Hunks* more than once or twice and lived through it. A quick drop by the toy store for a couple of genuine Junior Ranger badges, and the ensemble was complete.

"So," I explained, "Jane said Jimmy went MIA three days ago. Hubby and his goons should be back tonight, and we can make a social call."

"What's this 'we' shit, Batman?" Caretaker growled, "You got a mouse in yer pocket?"

"Ah, FWC gave me two shirts. I figure you can wear one." I said. "We're both about the same size, and your eyes often spot stuff I never even notice.

Caretaker held his arms out. Hey, I'm comfortable in this body," he pointed out. "What's wrong with this 'body size'?"

"You could eat hay and tow a Budweiser wagon," I pointed out, deadpan. "I was just saying the shirt won't hang on you like a tent when we go over there."

"Hey," Caretaker answered, "Just sayin, it's *your* shirt, fatty. And must I point out, I never actually said I was going along with this charade. By the way, what's the penalty for impersonating a Federal Officer? I have associates, or at least former associates, that would frown on me committing a felony."

"A Fish and Wildlife Inspector ain't exactly a 'Federal officer' position," I answered. "Besides, it's not like the dock will be crawling with inspectors at three in the morning." I wagged a finger. "We just pay a social call, ask if they have anything to declare, and send them on their happy way. "Anyway," I added, "Your eyes see

25

things I never even notice. Besides," I said finally, "You got anything better to do at three in the morning?"

"I have lots to do at three in the morning." This time, the snarl sounded a little dangerous. "Mostly snoring and staring at the inside of my eyelids."

"So come by the houseboat at two in a few days?" I answered, ignoring. He got up from his drink, left a tip on the table, and walked away without answering.

I waited three days and texted Caretaker. *"Showtime. Meet me at the houseboat around one tonight. We can walk across the street and pay a social call when he returns".*

He didn't answer.

A little after one in the morning, I heard the soft sound of a Timberline hiking boot bumping the door. "It's open!" I answered from my Lazyboy.

"Hands are full," came a muffled answer. I got up, twisted the knob and Caretaker pushed the door open with a Dunkin Donut coffee in each hand and a scowl that would make Chuck Norris cringe. Jake buried his nose in Caretaker's pocket, rooting for the Pupperoni dog treat he knew his friend would have.

"Where's this monkey suit you want me to wear?" Handing me a cup, he nodded, "Cream and sugar in that one." Holding up the other, he added, I like mine like I like my women."

"Black?" I questioned.

"Hot, wet, and steamy," he answered.

I shrugged.

There are four kinds of coffee in the world: Java, joe, jamoke, and carbon remover. Dunkin' coffee at one in the morning is somewhere between grades three and four. I took a sip, burned my tongue, spat the grounds out in the sink, and poured the rest down the toilet.

I laid two shirts out on the bed and offered one to him. He slipped it on over his semi-clean T-shirt, looking disgusted in the process. I pinned the Junior Firefighter pin on the shirt pocket and added a hat after letting the size out an inch.

"There. Nobody will notice what it really is. Try to stay out of any bright light."

"Hey, I'm happy just to stay right here in the houseboat, keep Jake company, and let you do this solo," he remarked, looking down at the little plastic badge. "I sure hope it's dark," he muttered.

I knew he would come along.

A little before two, the three of us walked away from Houseboat Row and crossed the street to the Bight. Caretaker raised his eyes toward the dog when I snapped on his leash. "Watchdog," I answered. "He can see and hear things, especially at night, that you and I wouldn't even pick up." Before we got to the dock, Jake let out a low "woof," and a few minutes later, the burble of twin diesels at idle speed came into earshot. While the crew was tying up and storing their gear in the cabin, I strode up to slack tide with a flashlight, clipboard, and pen in hand. The big electric reels, terminal tackle, and deepwater rods told me what they had been out for before they said anything.

Swordfish.

For the uneducated, the swordfish is found in deep water during the day and shallow depths at night when it comes closer to the surface to hunt. Considered a

27

warm-water species, the swordfish has a wide temperature tolerance, thanks to its "brain heater", a large bundle of tissue that insulates and warms the brain.

A popular sportfishing and commercial species, they are a mainstream item in seafood restaurants, though maybe a little less popular once mercury was found frequently in swordfish in the 90's. Swordfish usually range between fifty and two hundred pounds, although brutes over a thousand pounds have been boated.

There you go, as much as you will ever need to know (*and probably more*) about swordfish.

I cleared my throat. "Ah, evening, gentlemen. Agents Wahl and Falkenburg (*I could feel Caretaker cringe behind me),* Fish and Wildlife. Any luck tonight?"

All three crew members' heads snapped around in unison. "Uh, not a thing." One of the crewmembers mumbled. "Swordfishing tonight. Not a single bite." The crew was peering toward me, but I kept the flashlight pointed at them, partially so they couldn't see me and so I could see if anything looked suspicious.

"It's been slow lately," one of the others offered, in a Latin accent. All three were burly, tattooed, heavily muscled, bald-headed in sleeveless tank tops, and looked dangerous. One was black, one looked Latino, and I would guess the white guy was Jimmy.

"I've caught a few here and there," I commented. "Whadaya using for bait?"

He shrugged, nodding toward a big Yeti Cooler on the deck. I surmised he was Jimmy, Jane's husband, and the skipper. "We try it all, fresh bonito, mackerel, squid, lures, you never know when one of them brutes will hook up."

"Where are you fishing?" I asked.

The skipper pointed vaguely toward the east and south. "Oh, here and there, mostly out in the Gulfstream," he said, vaguely. "You know how it is. Sometimes we get lucky, sometimes not."

I noticed that Jimmy was wearing heavy rubber gloves. He noticed that I noticed. "My wife doesn't like the smell of fish," he explained. I wear these when I'm handling bait. It just gets to be a habit." He peered into the flashlight. "Will that be all, officers? We've been out for three days. I've got a shower, breakfast, and a soft bed in my future."

I flipped the light off. "Of course, gentlemen," I answered. "Have a good night." We walked away, back up the dock, while the crew finished tying up *Slack Tide*. We crossed the street and back to the houseboat.

Sitting down at the little table in the kitchen, I took out my pen and started making notes on the clipboard, a habit I learned from my father. You wrote down everything you noticed, even if it appeared inconsequential.

I wrote a number 1. "Thoughts?" I queried Caretaker. "For one, rubber gloves to keep the fish smell off?" he asked. "That sounded like you still wear a condom two days after doing the deed. I've never fished for swordfish, but I would hazard they ain't exactly two miles offshore."

I made a note. "My thoughts exactly," I replied. "The 'keep the smell from bothering your wife' like stinks like last week's mackerel. What else?"

"Well," Caretaker said slowly, "I'm no fisherman, but from what I could tell by flashlight, that boat looks like it hadn't boated a fish since Bush was President. Spotless."

I agreed and wrote that down, too. Caretaker stood up and looked at his Rolex. "I've enjoyed as much of this as I can stand, and I'm long overdue for a sportnap." Before closing the door behind him, he turned. "Call me when you want to get together. Preferably after Thanksgiving, or better yet, Christmas."

Wayne Gales

6

We were sitting at our "workplace" at *Hunks*, and I was staring at my phone, thinking that it had been almost a week since I had heard from Jane. I almost dropped it when it chirped, and I saw her number show. I thumbed to answer and switched the volume to speaker. "He's gone again." I could sense she was crying. "Fishing or not, I still think Jimmy and his friends are up to no good. Can you and Mr. Caretaker meet me somewhere? I'm not much of a drinker, but I could use a glass of wine to settle my nerves."

I glanced toward Caretaker and got a tiny headshake, "No". He made his finger into little legs and made a pillow with his hands and put them to the side of his face. I flipped the speaker off and put the phone to my ear. "Caretaker can't make it tonight. It's dark, Jane, and riding around town on your bike at night can't be safe. Can I pick you up?"

"Then why don't you just come by the townhouse?", she countered. "I have some wine here. We can sit on the porch and chat for a while. Will that be okay?"

"I can do that. What's your address?" I put her address in my map, took a last sip of my Mojito, and nodded to Caretaker. "I'll take notes and let you know tomorrow if I learn anything." He didn't answer, but just turned back to his drink in silence. I walked away thinking to myself, I wasn't looking for permission anyway.

Take that, old man.

The townhouse was on a quiet street in New Town. Jane was sitting on the porch in an Adirondack chair next to an unopened bottle of red wine. The hair on the back of my neck stood up a little when I recalled the last time a woman offered me a drink. It ended with six stab wounds and an extended stay in the Lower Keys Medical Center.

The wine was unopened. Two glasses, actually stemless wine glasses, sat on the table next to an opener. I opened the wine, poured, and, out of instinct and caution, reached for the furthest glass, looking to see if there was any reaction from her. She picked up the other glass, clinked a toast, and took a sip, wrinkling her nose in the process.

"Sorry, I'm such a lightweight when it comes to alcohol," she admitted. "But I'm just a wreck, worrying about what Jimmy might be up to. I thought a glass of wine might help me settle my nerves."

I gingerly tasted my glass, nodded approval, and picked up the bottle. "I'm not sure where you got it, but it's a damn good Merlot. I'm not a huge wine drinker myself, but when I do, I appreciate good wine." Jane smiled, something I rarely saw. Behind that plain facade was a beautiful person. I took another sip.

I set my wine down, leaned over the table, and kissed her.

I've been called a lot of things, but never smart. That move could have gone many ways, most of them bad.

One, she was still a client. Despite my offer to work *pro bono*, she insisted on paying me every week for the time I spent. Two, she didn't look exactly "come-hither". I could hardly believe she was straight and would have even the slightest interest in my advance.

And three…she was married.

Jane not only didn't resist, but she returned the kiss hungrily, passionately, and added a little tongue. I sat back down, took a big drink of wine, and looked toward the street apprehensively. She correctly interpreted my glance.

"Oh, I wouldn't worry, Brody," Jane said softly, "Jimmy never comes home early and is always gone two or three days." She started to cry softly. "I'm alone for days at a time!"

I stood up and took her into my arms, kissing her again. "Not anymore."

Jane pulled away a little, took me by the hand, and opened the door to lead me inside. She read my concern again. Lifting her dress, she pointed to a recent scar. "Hysterectomy six months ago," She reassured me. "I can't get pregnant."

I couldn't help but also notice she possessed neither underwear nor pubic hair. I'd always wondered if her tail was the same color as her mane.

I guess that mystery will remain a mystery.

Wayne Gales

7

My adult beverage meet-ups with Caretaker at our "office" at *Hunks* most afternoons became a little less frequent. If Caretaker noticed, he didn't mention it for a few weeks. One afternoon, he commented dryly, "Thinking with that little head again, Skippy? Her husband and his hoodlum buddies don't exactly look like Boy Scouts. They look more like extras from The Shawshank Redemption. I'll assume your junior private eye career is on hold for now?"

"I don't recall punching a time clock," I answered, looking into my mojito. "Oh, I'm still available if you have a need, just maybe not as much every night."

He turned toward me and cautioned, "I'll bring flowers to your grave. That is, if they can find enough of you to bury."

"Whaaat?" I answered, a little defensively. "I'm just comforting a client in distress."

He answered with a grumble, wiping the drink from his bushy mustache. "You and your dick, you mean."

He dropped the conversation there and went back to his drink.

I might have been a little over-defensive, but what he brought up had been on my mind. I did a little Amazon shopping, and a few days later, I called

Caretaker. He answered the phone with, "Need me to bring you flowers yet?"

"No, smartass," I answered. "I need to pay a little daytime visit to *Slack Tide*. Care to join? I need your attention to detail again."

"There's a Doctor Pimple Popper rerun this afternoon that sounds much more appetizing," he growled. "Why do you need me to hold your hand?"

"For one thing, I need to install a little device, and I don't want anyone to notice," I responded. "And, I need a lookout."

"And backup in a shootout?" he answered, hopefully.

"No guns," I cautioned. "I only have to be on the boat a minute or two."

Early afternoon at Garrison Bight is a quiet place. The half-day boats are already back, the full-day boats are still out, and sunset booze cruises are either hours away from boarding or located far away off Duval Street. After lunch at *Schooner Wharf* for a few beers and a couple of dozen oysters, we took the Jeep back to the houseboat, crossed Palm Avenue, and strolled down the dock toward *Slack Tide*. Looking left and right to make sure nobody was around, I stepped onto the deck while Caretaker kept an eye out for any company. I looked around for a likely spot, reached into my pocket, and attached a small disc under the fighting chair. It stuck with a resounding 'click'. Taking out my phone, I opened a program and nodded with satisfaction.

"Whadaya got?" Caretaker quizzed. "Microphone? Camera? C-4 explosives to get hubby out of the picture so you can have all that pussy to yourself?"

"GPS tracker, smart-ass," I answered. "It tracks the path and location of this tub anywhere in the world. I can set an electronic 'fence' around the boat, and anytime it moves more than fifty feet, my phone beeps. I know when it's leaving, where it's going, and when it's coming home. I bought two, so all I have to do is swap it out every few weeks or so, and *Slack Tide* has twenty-four-hour surveillance." I added smugly, "Now I will know where he's supposedly going to fish."

"How convenient." Caretaker added, "You put the bell on the cat. It will tell you when it's time to crawl out of Plain Jane's bed, put your shorts on, crawl out the bedroom window, and hightail it home, thereby extending your lazy life on this rock a few more days."

I didn't add that point, but the thought did cross my mind.

A few days later, my phone chirped. "He's gone again," Jane said.

"I know."

"How?"

"Better I show you."

The phone was silent for a moment, then she answered in a soft voice, just two words.

"Door's unlocked."

After three hours of uninhibited monkey sex, we took a break, and I showed Jane the app on my phone. "See, you can track the path and location of your hubby's boat." I sped the playback time up to eight times its normal speed. The little icon, was a truck and not a boat, since the usual application was for following a fleet of delivery vehicles. *Slack Tide* motored out of Garrison Bight and the keys in a south-easterly direction for a little more than three hours, and stopped. I jotted down the longitude and latitude, thumbed off the app for a moment, and looked online at a nautical map.

"Hmm," I said to myself, "A little south of Cay Sal Bank."

"They are at a bank?" Jane asked. "They're robbing a bank in the middle of the ocean?"

I chuckled.

"It's not the kind of bank you put money in," I explained. "Cay Sal Bank is a huge shallow area, mostly a big sand bar and a few islands, all uninhabited." I was a little curious about the *Slack Tide* location. "I suppose you could catch swordfish in deeper water out there, but it's legally Bahamian waters, so you would need a permit from the Bahama government along with the usual Florida licenses, but…" My thoughts trailed off.

"But what?" Jane asked.

"But, along with those permissions, you are dangerously close to Cuba. Cuban patrol boats might hassle you that close to their northern coast." I clicked back to the GPS tracker. Slack tide was still stationary.

"It's still daylight," I looked out the window. "Swordfish stay deep during the day and come closer to the surface at night to feed." I clicked off the phone. "We wait." Jane slid an arm across my bare chest. "I have an idea how we can pass the time," She purred.

Eight p.m. came and went, and the little blip didn't move, then nine, ten, midnight. *Slack Tide* stayed in the same location. "Whatever they are doing, it's not fishing for swordfish," I commented, almost to myself. And the gear I saw them stowing that night was all deep water gear." I thumbed off the app again and set the phone on the table. That boat hasn't moved all night." Jane put my face in her hands and kissed me. "Stay until morning?" she implored, almost pleading. "We can go to coffee at *Blue Heaven*. I don't eat breakfast, but I'm sure you do."

Looking at her tiny body, A cup breasts, and a waistline I could almost circle with my hands, I commented, "It doesn't look like you eat breakfast, lunch, or dinner." I felt like I was sleeping with a twelve-year-old, a thought that skeeved me out, making me almost unable to perform.

Almost.

After breakfast, I noted slack tide was moving again, going northwest toward Key West at about fifteen knots I showed the movement to Jane, dropped her off at her townhouse, and headed to the houseboat for some sleep, an necessity I dearly loved and was unable to enjoy the previous night, but not before walking Jake, who scolded me with his big brown eyes for having to sleep alone last night.

This dance continued for almost two months. Slack tide always went near the same location, and just sat for a few days, before returning to Key West, apparently always empty-handed. Jane had stopped paying me since week two. Hell, I felt I should be paying *her*.

The lovemaking was intense and fun, and I had a perfect way to keep tabs on her husband. One morning, while she was dressing, she sat on the bed. "This can't go on forever, you know."

"You mean, the sex?" I asked. "Heck, I can go on this way for a long time, unless you are getting tired of me."

"No, no, not that," she answered. "You need to find out what he's really up to. If he's doing something illegal, I don't want to get caught up in it. What can you do?"

"I'm not sure," I answered, shaking my head. "I've watched them come back into the harbor, and haven't seen anything illegal, just three fishermen with either poor skills or bad luck. If I saw something, I could call the cops, but they won't arrest someone based on my suspicion that they might be doing something outside the law."

Jane looked lost in thought for a moment. "What if you tailed them out to where they go and try to see what they are doing?"

"It's not like I can hide behind a tall building out there," I replied. "I've been there, looking at abandoned buildings with my dad. There's nothing around Cay Sal Bank more than five feet above sea level. I would be as conspicuous as a nun in a whorehouse." I looked at the nautical map on Jane's laptop for a few minutes and had an idea.

"Perhaps I can head out that way a day in advance, and hide behind a low Key. I don't think I could see much at night, but maybe I could see if something suspicious was going on." I thumbed my phone to make a call. "I know someone with night binoculars. I'll see if I can borrow them."

Wayne Gales

8

Interlude;
Cay Sal Bank History

The Caribbean had its first taste of Spanish timber on Christmas Day 1492, when Christopher Columbus' flagship, the Santa María, sank off the coast of what is now Haiti. Over the following four centuries, as Spain's maritime empire swelled, peaked, and collapsed, the Caribbean devoured hundreds of ships and thousands of people, swallowing gold, silver, emeralds, and other priceless treasures to the deep.

Nearly 700 shipwrecks off Cuba, Panama, the Dominican Republic, Haiti, Bermuda, the Bahamas, and the U.S. Atlantic coast have been documented.

Its inventory runs from the sinking of Columbus' flagship to July 1898, when the Spanish destroyer *Plutón* was hit by a U.S. boat off Cuba, heralding the end of the Spanish-American War and the twilight of Spain's imperial age. Archaeologists and treasure seekers have located the remains of fewer than a quarter of those vessels to date.

Treasure hunters tend to be more interested in ships that came to grief on their way back from the Americas to Spain, as they were often burdened with treasure, but ill-fated outward-bound vessels are just as compelling.

The findings go beyond cutlasses and crucifixes and help to explain how Spain succeeded in enriching itself for centuries. Tons of mercury was sent to the New World by Spain to be used in extracting gold and silver from the mines that fed the empire, along with clothes for slaves and weapons to be used in putting down local rebellions.

Cay Sal, meaning "Salt Cay" in Spanish, is located fifty-five miles south of Marathon in the Florida Keys. Cay Sal is south of Cuba and close to the Gulf Stream, the established route for Galleons traveling to Spain. A property of the Bahamas, Cay Sal and the 2000 square mile Cay Sal Bank's shallow waters have made for a treacherous location for ships straying from established routes.

Cay Sal was discovered during early exploration of the New World and is depicted on many of the first maps. The island has an interior lagoon where sea salt could be easily produced by solar evaporation, and there are records of the Spanish doing just that. An 1824 English map also shows "Salt Rakers Huts" on the island when it was a British possession. Salt was in great demand as a preservative before refrigeration; it was used to preserve meat, seafood, and many other commodities.

In 1839 a lighthouse was built by England's Imperial Lighthouse Service 15 miles north of Cay Sal on Elbow Cay. The location was strategic to Gulf Stream shipping, warning vessels off the Bank, which has claimed countless shipwrecks over the years. The remains of ships can still be occasionally seen in shallow water.

Wayne Gales

9

I called Walter, one of the dockhands at the Bight, to bring *Whisper* to life. "Top her off and fill the potable water, Walter," I instructed, then, remembering the episode when I nearly died, *(and got laid),* I added, with a grim smile, "Make sure both batteries are charged and strong, They don't push-start very well in the middle of the ocean."

"Do you want the chests filled with ice and drinks?" Walter asked", sounding hopeful. I could tell he was jonesing for a big tip.

"Not yet," I answered. "I'm going out soon, but not sure when. Ah, it depends on the moon and tides and such." My trip *really* depended on when slack tide was going out, but Walter didn't need to know that part.

"Going by yourself, Mr. Brody?" Walter was wondering if I was going to bring along another plus-10 eye candy body with me, like Lexi Sawyer.

"Nope, just Jake and me." I could almost see the disappointment in Walter's face.

I started making preparations at home, picking up a dozen pieces of fried chicken from Dion's Quick Mart, along with some Gatorade and bottled water, then made a "go kit", putting a dog dish and a few survival items in a bag. If Jake saw that I packed his dish, he made no notice of it, but lay sound asleep in a sunbeam in front of the sliding glass door. But I knew that he knew. Not much escaped Jake's eye, even if they appeared closed. I had already contacted the Bahamian government and secured a Bahamas fishing license. Since I was going to be out there for a few days, it wouldn't hurt to have a reason for being there and put a few dolphin or grouper in the chest along the way.

Later in the week, I got a one-word text from Jane. "Tonight." I called Walter and told him to add ice to the chests, gathered my stuff, and opened the door. Jake got up, stretched lazily, and trotted out the door in front of me. He knew where we were going and didn't need a leash. I was a little reluctant to take him on a trip that might last two or three days, but he couldn't stay here by himself that long, and anyway, he was good company and loved Dion's fried chicken, as long as I pulled the meat off the bones.

It was a five-minute walk to *Whisper*. Jake greeted Walter with a tail wag, jumped into the boat, and assumed his position, perched on the bow like a cross between a hood ornament and Leonardo DiCaprio in *Titanic*. We idled out of Garrison Bight and brought Whisper up to speed. I set a course for Cotton Cay on the southern end of Cay Sal Banks, the island closest to where *Slack Tide* seemed to hang out on its trips. Cruising at a comfortable twenty-four knots, we got to the area in less than three hours. Walter had put a small bag of frozen shiners in the ice chest, and after slowing down and shutting off *Whisper*, I let the boat drift while I baited up.

Far from any heavily fished areas, Cay Sal Bank should be a target-rich environment, but my depth finder wasn't marking any fish, and what looked like a flat, sandy bottom fifty feet under me made for poor fishing. We drifted along with the current for a half hour until I started marking fish, and the bottom showed a little structure. I pushed Jake out of the way, opened the bow hatch, and threw the anchor. *Whisper* obediently pulled around into the current as the anchor caught. I boated a few yellowtail, one lively dolphin, and a twenty-pound Nassau grouper. "That's enough fun," I announced to Jake. "I would guess you could use a little dry land about now."

He wagged his tail in agreement. I untied the anchor and pulled. Whatever it had caught on had it caught good. I had an app for that. I pulled a big float out of the bow hatch and attached it to the anchor line.

Tying one end firmly to a cleat, I powered up and headed in the opposite direction to the current, a trick that always works. The power drives the big float underwater, and the buoyancy pulls the anchor away. I took off, and instead of the float coming to the surface with the anchor, the *Whisper* lurched to a stop and spun around. I tried again from several directions with the same results.

I had over three hundred bucks invested in the anchor, about ten feet of chain, and a few hundred feet of good line, and I didn't want to just abandon it. "Well, Jake, I'll just have to go down and see what it's hooked on, but not today." Jake's eyes seemed to agree with my wisdom. Anyway, I didn't have any scuba gear on board and no enthusiasm for leaving *Whisper* alone with nobody but a dog in charge while I free-dived fifty feet.

Untying the line, I attached a gallon milk jug to it and motored away. As reluctant as I was to leave my property there if I couldn't raise the anchor, nobody else could with anything smaller than a big shrimp boat.

We were a few miles from Cotton Cay, and I beached *Whisper* on the side of the island away from open seas, using a sand spike to secure the boat. It was a long way from the mainland on a little dry island. If

Whisper floated away, it could be weeks or months before they found our dry, dead bodies. Jake happily jumped ashore and went out of sight, exploring.

I knew he couldn't go far. Jake came back after a half hour with that, *"Why aren't you exploring with me?"* look. I looked at the sun getting low on the horizon and decided it was time to get in position. Gathering a few drinks, the night vision binocs, and my cooler much to Jake's delight, and set out for the open-water side of Cotton Cay. Plopping down on the sandy beach, we shared cold fried chicken and waited… for *something*.

Wayne Gales

10

And waited. And waited. Finally, around midnight, Jake perked up his ears and gave a low, "Woof!" Maybe a half hour later, I heard the quiet rumble of twin diesels, and saw the faint trail of phosphorescent water, typical in tropical waters, in the distance, and saw a boat come to a stop. Even with the infrared binocs, I could only make out faint objects that far away. The only thing I could really determine was that I had fished over that exact same area the day before, and that area is far too shallow for Swordfishing, even at night.

I continued to watch the boat throughout the night, but it appeared to stay motionless, dark, and quiet. Jake and I went back to *Whisper* just before dawn, and while he curled up on the bow, I threw a few cushions on the deck and flaked out for a few hours.

Shortly after sunrise, we walked back to the beach and had the rest of our cold chicken for breakfast. *Slack Tide* hadn't moved, and with my good Rico 'regular' binoculars, I could tell there wasn't a single line in the water. I was about to call this excursion a bust when Jake stood up, looked toward the south, and gave another quiet 'woof'. With the binocs, I could pick out another boat in the distance. It was too far away to tell what kind of vessel, but it was obviously heading toward *Slack Tide*. It slowed and nestled up to the larger boat. Unintelligible voices drifted across the water. I could only make out a little laughter. Presently, the little boat pulled away and motored off into the distance.

Toward Cuba.

"Well, Jake," the big dog perked up, hearing his name. "I think we have learned everything we can learn about this event."

Nothing.

I headed back to Key West, swinging well north so *Slack Tide* wouldn't see *Whisper*. When I got to port, I cleaned my catch and instructed the dock hand, "Freshen her up, I'm heading back out in the morning." Walter admired my catch. I'm sure he was hoping I would share a little. "Looks like you done good, Brody. Whatcha goin out for tomorrow?" Handing Walter a big grouper filet, the answer puzzled him.

"My anchor."

I didn't really want to dive without a buddy, but all my friends were occupied, so I called for the next best thing, a crewman. The phone rang twice before Caretaker answered. "All your body parts intact?" he said sarcastically, "Or do I need to bring a needle, thread, and a box of Band-aids?"

"Very funny," I answered. "I just need someone to come with me back out to Cay Sal Bank in the morning. My anchor got stuck under something."

"The only boat I plan to get on has five bars, a gourmet restaurant, a few dozen teenagers in bikinis with thong bottoms lounging by the pool, and a bevy of desperate, horny, blue-haired grandmas throwing their room keys at me."

"I just need you to ride along so I don't leave *Whisper* unattended," I said.

"Oh, and a name that ends with 'Of the Seas,'" Caretaker completed. "Don't you have a bunch of Bubbas that can do this? If I had my druthers, I'd druther not."

"Everyone else is busy," I explained, "And I don't want that anchor to end up on someone else's boat. Come on, my friend, it's just a half-day's ride."

"Ok, one short trip," he answered. "But it will cost you a lobster dinner."

"How about stuffed grouper with sauteed portobello mushrooms and Caesar salad, prepared tableside?"

"I can go for that, I guess," Caretaker conceded. "Sounds fancy. Where are we going?"

"I'll surprise you," I said with a little grin. "Just come to the houseboat Sunday afternoon."

Dad taught me a little cooking in his later days.

Caretaker, Jake, and I headed out the next morning, with my dog standing at the bow with a big smile and his ears blowing in the wind. The Florida straits were glassy smooth at sunrise, and I was able to bump *Whisper* up to a quick thirty knots.

Using the GPS, I slowed down when we got near the place where I'd lost my anchor, and after putting around the area for fifteen minutes, I spotted the floating milk jug. I pulled up the anchor line tight and tied it to a cleat, then put my tank, mask, fins, and weight belt on. Nodding to Caretaker, I said, "I'll be back in a jiffy", put the regulator in my mouth, and flipped backward off the boat.

Diving solo is never smart. I've been called a lot of things, but never smart. But hey, you wanna live forever? After all, it's only fifty feet down in crystal-clear water as warm as a bathtub. Heck, if I looked hard enough, I could almost see the anchor down there and whatever it was stuck under.

Almost.

I pulled myself down the anchor line to the bottom and up to the anchor. I tugged at the chain. It was definitely stuck.

Under a cannon.

I took my knife out of the leg sheath and scraped at some of the encrustations. I couldn't tell for sure, but it definitely wasn't modern, probably 17th century.

Well, I'll be dipped in shit.

You hunt for years, sometimes decades, for a hint, just a hint, of finding a wreck, and I just stuck my anchor under one by accident. Where there's a cannon, there's probably a whole shipwreck nearby.

I surfaced and handed my gear up to Caretaker, one piece at a time. He untied the rope from the deck cleat and started pulling, assuming I had freed the anchor. I gave a 'halt' sign and climbed the ladder back into *Whisper*.

"Give me the line. I'm going to tie the milk jug back on." With a grin, I added, "You will never believe what that anchor is jammed under." Spooling up the motors, I spun *Whisper* around and brought the boat back up to speed while I explained to Caretaker what I found.

"So, you're back in the treasure business?", asked Caretaker while he held the rails to the Bimini top to keep from going swimming. I had the boat at full speed now. I had to tell somebody the news. Despite the gentle swell, Jake kept his desired position at the bow. His balance looked effortless.

Answering Caretaker's question, I held up my phone. "Not me, I don't have the boat or the equipment to mount a serious effort, and I don't even know how to get permission from the Bahamian government to initiate a salvage effort, but I know somebody that might, and I'm calling as soon as we get back to port."

"Does he live in Key West?", Caretaker asked.

"No," I answered, and it's a *her*".

Helen answered the phone on the first ring, "Brody! Tell me you are in Sebastian! I have a fresh bottle of Jameson to share! Come on over!"

Helen O'Rourke had a cover band in the Keys years ago, and Dad used to sit in with them occasionally. The band, called Helen Wait and the Waiters, was a popular group with a big following. The standing joke was that if anyone had a complaint, request, or even wanted to hear "Free Bird", bandmembers would point at their lead singer and tell them to go to "Hell and Wait". Dad said that as a band leader, she was a cross between Mother Theresa and Darth Vader.

Leading a band is not a vocation for the timid.

I worked for Helen briefly when she found and salvaged one of the 1715 wrecks, pulling hundreds of pounds of silver out of the waters east of Sebastian Inlet. My mother died when I was pretty young, and Helen helped fill that void in my heart. She was thirty years older than me, but she stopped having birthdays, so eventually I'll catch up. It was good to hear her voice.

"No, Helen, I'm in Key West still. I found something today that might interest you." Her voice turned from motherly love to cold businesswoman in an instant.

"What now?", Helen said with a touch of sarcasm. "Another wild goose chase like we did under the seven-mile bridge?"

I explained that when I went down to recover a stuck anchor, I discovered it was hung up under what looked like an ancient cannon. Her questions came fast and furious. "When? Where? How deep? Does that spot show on any existing wreck sites? Can you find it again?"

I told her I found it earlier this morning, that it was in fifty feet of water off Cotton Cay on Cay Sal Bank, and no, I didn't see it anywhere on any existing sites.

"Can you find it?" Helen asked. "The sands around there shift with the currents all the time. I have heard more than once of someone finding a wreck only to have it disappear in a day."

"I left the anchor stuck under that cannon, with a hundred feet of line and a milk jug still attached," I answered. "And I have the GPS coordinates. We can find it in minutes."

Instead of directly answering, Helen mused over the phone. "Cotton Cay, that's Bahamas territory. We'll need to file with Nassau. I've never done it, and I hear it's quite a process, but I know the basics". The next thing she said wasn't especially to me, but to herself.

"What comes first, the chicken or the egg? You can't file for salvage rights unless you have something to salvage, and how do you know, unless you start working the site?" She answered herself with the next step. "Can you meet me there in a day or so? I'll bring *Hoedown* and drop the mailboxes for a little snooping. No recovering, just a little snooping. You can't get in trouble for snooping, can you?"

"You can't if you don't get caught," I answered.

I doubt many Bahamian officials cruise that neighborhood very often. Her volunteering to bring the *Hoedown* and hover over "my cannon" gave me an idea.

"I have a few things to clear up before I can go out again," I explained. "Can I call you when I can meet?"

"Of course," Helen reassured me. "Just let me know, and I'll head toward Cotton Cay."

Hoedown was a big boat, over forty-five feet in length, with a flying bridge and two "mailboxes" in back. Invented in 1962 by treasure hunting great Mel Fisher, mailboxes are huge curved tubes that could be swung under a boat, diverting the propeller thrust. Props that normally propel a boat would force propwash directly down and blow away sand and overburden, hopefully exposing wreckage and treasure. While I was sure the mailboxes would help us find a wreck, that twenty-foot-high bridge had a more immediate interest to me, and maybe give me a better look at *Slack Tide* and its shenanigans.

After hanging up with Helen, I realized I had a Jake problem. Turning to Caretaker, I casually asked, "Care to have a furry bed partner for a few days?"

"I overheard your call," he muttered sarcastically. "It sounds like you are going to be back out there for a few days." Casually scratching Jake behind the ears, Caretaker nodded. "I'll babysit Jake anytime. You don't need to ask, just drop him off."

Wayne Gales

11
Interlude;
Salvaging Cay Sal Bank

There are numerous stories about recreational divers coming across ancient cannons near Cay Sal Bank. Often uncovered after a recent storm, they would be unable to find them later under shifting sands. If one were to find debris, the steps to salvage it are difficult and time-consuming.

Cay Sal Bank is within the Bahamas' territorial waters, and permission would have to be obtained from the Bahamian authorities. The Bahamas has an agreement with the U.S. Coast Guard to regularly monitor Cay Sal Bank, including Cay Sal, one would need to contact the Bahamas Ministry of Transport or the Bahamian Coast Guard to request permission and navigate the salvage process, as the Bahamian authorities would be responsible for granting any salvage rights. You will be required to provide information about the vessel, the nature of the salvage, and any relevant documentation. Only after that, a formal request for permission to salvage the property would need to be submitted, explaining the situation and the actions planned.

This will likely involve demonstrating that there is a legitimate need for salvage and that you have the expertise and resources to do so safely.

At that point, the Bahamian authorities would negotiate the terms of the salvage, including who would be responsible for the salvage operation, how the salvaged property would be managed, and how any salvage reward would be determined. Compliance with all applicable Bahamian laws and regulations related to salvage, including environmental protection and maritime safety, would be required.

Finally, while the Bahamas manages salvage operations within its waters, the U.S. Coast Guard might still have a role in assisting with the salvage permitting process, especially if there is a U.S. citizen involved or if the salvage operation impacts U.S. waters or vessels.

Since the area is located less than thirty miles from Cuba, the possibility of running afoul of the Cuban authorities is always a risk. History has shown that Cuba and their Russian-built patrol boats don't always play nice.

Unless they are on your side.

Wayne Gales

12

I got the heads up from Jane that Jimmy would be out of the house in two nights. As much as a conjugal visit sounded appetizing, I called Helen with the news instead. She agreed to head toward Cotton Cay with a crew as soon as she loaded provisions.

I got out to the site early the next morning. *Hoedown* had already found my milk jug and had divers in the water. "You don't waste time," I remarked, pulling up and tying *Whisper* off on Hellen's boat.

"I sent the boys down to rescue your anchor, and to look around," she explained. "Then we're going to blow the site with the mailboxes to see if anything else shows."

"Good plan," I agreed. "I'll just be a spectator."

Helen put her hands on her hips. "You mean you're not going to join the fun? That's not the Brody Wahl I know." She held her arms wide. "Where's your dive gear?" I admitted my tank, fins, mask, and regulator were with me. "I just didn't want to get in your way," I said.

"Nonsense," Helen answered with a big smile. "Get your gear. I plan to pay you a share *if* we find anything and *if* the Bahamian Government lets us salvage, and that's a couple of big 'ifs'. Plan to get your ass in the water after we blow." This visit wasn't my real reason for coming, but Helen didn't need to know that, and it doesn't take a lot of coaxing to get me to dive, especially when I didn't have to dive solo.

A few minutes later, one of Helen's divers surfaced, holding the line to my anchor. "It's free, Brody," he instructed. "Pull away!" I brought my anchor up and stored it in the bow. The two divers surfaced, and after looking around to make sure nobody was in sight, we loosened the two big metal tubes and lowered them under the boat. "Technically," Helen explained, "we shouldn't be doing this without a salvage permit from the Bahamas, but how can you file for one if you don't know what you are salvaging for?" Powering up the *Hoedown*, Helen pushed the throttles up to cruising speed, focusing the boat's propwash straight down.

After a half-hour, she shut the twin diesels off again. "Okay, boys," Helen announced. "Fifteen-minute break to let any clouded water clear up, then down for a look."

It felt good to strap a tank on again. It had been a while. With a nod from the other two, we flipped backwards off the side of *Hoedown* and headed down. After the wait, the waters were bathtub warm and crystal clear.

The weight belt I had strapped on had slightly negative buoyancy to help me stay near the bottom while I was poking around any wreck site. I would have loved to bring along my big underwater metal detector, but that would have been frowned upon by the Bahamian Government should an official happen to be in the neighborhood.

The cannon was more exposed and clearly visible. The three of us beelined for the newly dug hole with the dream of picking up a gold chain or a handful of doubloons, but other than the cannon, nothing much else was visible. After another fifteen minutes of sweeping away sand with our hands, one of the crew tapped his tank with a knife handle, gave a "thumbs down" motion, and then pointed toward the surface. I nodded in agreement.   Just before working my way back to *Hoedown*, a black round rock caught my eye on the bottom. Looking it over, I couldn't tell if it was just a rock or something interesting.   It *was* about the right size and shape to be a coin, so I slipped it into my glove and surfaced.

Once on board, I handed the black rock to Helen. Like me, she turned it over and over in her hands.

"It sure looks like it could be a coin," she remarked. Helen moved toward the cabin. Holding the suspected coin in one hand in the air, she remarked, "Well, one way to find out quick." She emerged from the cabin with an empty Mason jar and a plastic bottle marked "poison – muriatic acid".   I nodded, understanding. The pool chemical is a good way to dissolve encrustation from silver. Setting the jar on a shelf with the "suspected coin" covered in the acid, Helen continued, "we'll know by morning." My experience agreed that in the morning, either a shiny eight reale coin would be in the jar or nothing at all.

That stuff is strong.

Wayne Gales

13

The GPS tracker on my phone didn't work out here – no cell service, but while everyone on *Hoedown* settled down for a hot meal (baloney on toast), I told Helen, "I think I'll climb up on the bridge and enjoy the scenery." She nodded, and I took my Ricohs with me up the stairs.

From that point, I had a commanding view of the area. It was almost three hours, nearly sunset, before I saw a boat in the distance. With the binoculars, I could tell by the hull color that it was probably *Slack Tide*. The fishing boat slowed to a stop, but only for a few minutes, then moved away to the west and south until it was no more than a speck in the distance. I would guess they didn't like *Hoedown's* proximity to their "normal" spot.

Oh well, so much for my brilliant plan. I made a bed in *Whisper* out of the seat cushions and drifted off to sleep.

Before leaving the next morning, Helen took the mason jar off the shelf, held the colander over the water and dumped out the contents. After washing it in salt water to get the acid off, she yelled, "Score!" and held up a shiny silver eight-reale coin. We passed the coin around. I'd held hundreds of similar coins in the past. "The coat of arms on one side and cross on the other means almost certainly seventeenth or eighteenth century," I noted. Helen agreed. "I don't see a date on it. I'd have to look under a microscope to figure out when it was minted and where. But, no matter," she added, with a sigh, "It will become the property of the Monarchy of the Bahamas the moment we present it with our salvage application." She put the coin in a plastic bag and secured it in a locked box.

"We'll keep you posted on developments," she said before pulling away from *Whisper*. "We have the location, pictures of the cannon, and the coin. I hope that's enough to get a permit."

We parted with a hug, then a wave.

What Happens in Key West…

Wayne Gales

14

A few weeks later, the GPS tracker software indicated on my phone that the battery was down to thirty percent, so after my go-to raw oyster lunch at Schooner Wharf, I drove back to the Houseboat. Popping the spare, charged-up GPS tracker in my pocket, I wandered over to Garrison Bight, stepping onto *Slack Tide* when nobody was in the area.

The swap-out was a two-minute process, just pulling one unit out from under the fighting chair and replacing it with a fresh one. No bigger than a silver dollar, I heard the unit make a solid "ker-chunk" sound when the magnetic tracker attached itself to the bottom of the chair.

Since nobody was in the area, I decided a little look around *Slack Tide* wouldn't hurt. I tried the cabin door, even though I was sure it would be locked, and rummaged through the drawers under the helm. There wasn't much left to examine. Before I got out of the boat, I lifted the lid of the big Yeti bait chest, leaned over, and took a big whiff. As I had already suspected, the bait chest didn't look like it ever held bait. The inside of the Yeti looked as clean as new, and there was no fishy smell at all. The only thing inside was one of the yellow Rubbermaid gloves Jimmy said he wore to keep the smell away from his wife. I picked up the glove, sniffed it, and even gave it a quick lick test. If there had ever been fish on that glove, I sure couldn't tell. Maybe they washed everything in Purex bleach after every trip, a step I would never partake in after a fishing outing.

"I don't know what they are doing or where they are going," I mumbled to myself, "But I don't think any fishing is involved." Throwing the glove back in the box, I closed and latched the lid, like I had found it. Climbing out of *Slack Tide*, I brushed off a little wave of nausea. I started to wonder if I'd consumed some bad oysters at my *Schooner Wharf* lunch. I started walking back to the houseboat, hoping I didn't hurl my lunch on the way.

I felt like a bucket full of dog turds, with all the good ones picked out. I've never had a bad oyster at *Schooner Wharf,* but I might have caught one today.

As I walked toward the houseboat, I started feeling worse and worse, and dizzy. Well, a few more minutes and I could lie down and take a little sport nap.

Fortunately, the houseboat was only across the street from Garrison Bight

Unfortunately, there was a busy street between me and Houseboat Row.

Fortunately, there was a crosswalk, where all the locals *(and most tourists)* stopped.

Unfortunately, I didn't make it all the way across Palm Avenue before I passed out.

Fortunately, I was sound asleep prior to face-planting on the white line in the middle of the street.

What Happens in Key West...

Wayne Gales

15

Not like I make it a habit, but during my last ambulance ride to *this* hospital, I was blissfully unconscious. This time, it was almost surreal. I felt like I was hovering above my body. An oxygen mask covered my face, an IV was stuck in my arm, and some sort of nasty spray was being shot into my nose. I wanted to sit up, get out of the gurney, and walk home, but I couldn't even move. I drifted off to sleep.

After what seemed like a hundred years, but was probably more like an hour, I came to in a hospital bed, staring at the ceiling, with an IV still in my arm and all kinds of wires stringing out of my blanket. The O2 mask was still over my face. I reached up with my free hand and pulled off the mask. With curtains on both sides and in front of me, I was sure I was in the emergency room at Lower Keys Medical Center.

I sensed, more than saw, someone was sitting in the room waiting for me to come around.

Caretaker.

"Texas déjà vu all over again." He started. "They saw my number on your phone with my name on the ID. Do you think I have nothing better to do than bring your lazy ass flowers?" I raised up on one elbow. "Thanks for picking the scab off that memory".

A few months ago, I was in Texas looking for lost Aztec treasure when a dude with a bad mullet and worse teeth tried to shoot me with an antique buffalo rifle. He didn't succeed, but we both tumbled off a cliff, dislocating my shoulder and killing him in the process.

Looking around, I commented, "I don't see any flowers, but a Wendy's single with cheese, fries, and a chocolate frosty would be welcome about now." I shook my head. "Man, those must have been some bad oysters. I've yakked up lunch a time or two in my day, but I don't think I've ever passed out."

Caretaker was holding a sheet of paper. He passed it to me. At first glance, it was a sheet of unintelligible medical terms. Handing it back, I asked, " Could you have someone translate this for me?"

Without looking at it, he mock-read it to me. "Drug overdose, my lad. Fentanyl in your bloodstream, probably not enough to kill you, but a sufficient dose to make you take a nap in the middle of Palm Avenue."

"Fentanyl?" I answered slowly. I don't take drugs, you know that. Never touched the stuff, never will." Sitting up, I pointed at the plastic bag hanging behind the door with my clothes and instructed, "Call the nurse and get this IV out of my arm, and all these things off my chest. I want to go home."

Caretaker pointed a finger at me. "Not so fast, Buckaroo. People want to talk to you."

They sure did. People, lots of people. First came the doctor, who poked, prodded, committed all kinds of indignities on my body, then left without a comment. Then came a couple of nurses, who, after more indignities, grudgingly, at my request (pleading), pulled out the IV, unhooked me from the monitors, and let me get dressed.

Shortly after, a social worker came by to educate me on the several therapy groups that regularly met to help me with "my problem". "I don't have a problem," I answered indignantly. "It must have been some kind of accident." She nodded with that motherly look that said, *"Sure, that's what they all say."*

I shut up; it wasn't worth the argument.

"Can I go?" I asked for the umpteenth time. "Not quite yet," the duty nurse answered. You have another visitor first."

Not visitor, but these were *visitors.* It must have been a slow day down at the Police Department. Four uniformed cops came into the room. I was hoping Uncle John would be among them, but either he was off or didn't want to pull the "family" chip.

They already had my ID, confirmed my address, and asked a zillion questions. Caretaker stood up, cleared his throat, pulled out his wallet, and showed them a *real* badge and a business card. "He works with me and i've never seen him take drugs. I can vouch for him." I'm not sure what Caretaker's badge was for. I knew he used to have some sort of government job, but I never knew what he did, but it appeared to pull some sort of weight with the local police. "We can let him go for now, but we are getting a warrant to search his house."

I reached into my pocket. "You don't need a warrant," I said, holding my keys. "I'll open the house for you. You won't find anything stronger than a bottle of Tylenol, and it's never been opened. And," I added, "I will need to come along and make sure Jake, my dog, plays nice. He doesn't welcome unknown visitors. Especially, if you bring a drug sniffing dog with you."

I was released, and they gave me a ride in the squad car. I wasn't allowed to ride with Caretaker so I wouldn't flee the country, like you could get five miles fleeing north on U.S.1. Caretaker *did* come and took

81

Jake on a long walk while they rummaged through my stuff, drug dog, and all.

"You know, Mr. Wahl, possession of as little as four grams of fentanyl could result in a five-year prison sentence and a five-thousand-dollar fine, but we can be lenient if you surrender any drugs. We will also search your boat shortly."

Since everyone assumed I was on drugs, I didn't bother to comment much, but this changed my mind, quick. "I think I know how I got poisoned." Everyone's head snapped around. "Ah, revelations, you suddenly remember." Said one officer. "Tell us."

We all sat down at the table while I explained. "Caretaker and I have a client (*that I'm banging*) who hired us to track a cheating husband (*true*). I learned that he was not cheating (*true*) but going fishing, but apparently not for fish, so I installed a GPS tracking device to see where he was going (*so I knew when I could bang her*). I watched them from a distance on a nearby island, and I'm sure they met up with a boat from the south, like Cuba. I'll bet that's where the drugs are coming from. After they got back, I was checking out his boat, and I must have come in contact with the fentanyl."

The Lieutenant chewed this for a moment. "Installing a tracking device on a vehicle without the owner's permission is a misdemeanor, and getting on his boat is trespassing. You may not be in trouble for drug possession, but it sounds like you are far from out of the woods." He continued. "I've had dealings with your father in the past, Mr. Wahl. It doesn't sound like the apple fell far from the tree."

He made some notes and continued. "At the same time, you *did* apparently suffer an accidental overdose while on that boat, and I think it gives us, the Coast Guard, or DEA, the permission to conduct an inspection. Where is this boat?" I took my phone out of my pocket and thumbed the tracking program. Holding it up for the cops to see, I pointed out, "According to this, *Slack Tide* is sitting about three miles west of Cay Sal Bank, in the Bahamas." The Lieutenant peered at the tracking, then made a call.

After hanging up, he instructed, "The Coast Guard has authority to board and search in that area, but I doubt they would, based on one person recovering from an overdose. Better yet, we wait for them to come back to Key West, especially if the Coasties see another boat rendezvousing with them from the south like you said."

Wayne Gales

16

Caretaker told me to give him a heads-up when *Slack Tide* was on the way from Cay Sal Bank, and he would alert the DEA. "They should be back about nine tonight," I advised him. "Ok," he texted back, "Meet me by *Whisper* about eight."

My boat was a dozen slips away from where Jones and his crew docked. I walked across the street, and not only my friend but a half dozen other people were hanging around, all in black outfits and bullet-proof vests, with a large 'DEA' logo on their backs. Everyone had sidearms in a holster and an ominous-looking rifle in hand.

I was a little surprised that Caretaker was wearing a nearly identical outfit, but no guns save a holstered pistol. I raised my eyebrows at his appearance.

"DEA?"

"It's a loaner vest since mine is in a Las Vegas storage unit. They don't expect any incident, just a confrontation and arrest with the goods, but the only people that have ever seen the perps are you and me, and I told them you had an aversion to things that go bang in the dark, so I volunteered." Pointing at the agent's weapons, he told me, "They are all carrying LAR-15 semi-automatic carbines if there's an incident." Pointing at his holster, he explained, "I've just got my forty five caliber Judge with a two inch barrel, not because I expect to use it, but both because I feel naked without it and it feels good to have it strapped on."

Everyone knows, especially Caretaker, that I have no personal use for guns. Never have, never will. All of his caliber and firearm designation lingo was just Greek to me. I nodded as if I understood every word and looked at my GPS. "*Slack Tide* is about a mile from here," I reported. One of the DEA agents clicked off his phone and nodded to me. "The Coasties have eyes-on," he agreed. Rounding up his crew, he pointed down the dock. Caretaker put his hand on my shoulder. "Wait here. We'll make the pinch, easy-peasy, and you can go home to bed. *Capiche?*"

I took a seat on my boat as the group walked partway in the dark toward *Slack Tide*, waiting until the boat was shut down and secured before making their arrest. It all went down according to plan.

Until it didn't.

I saw a bright flash of light followed by a large bang, breaking the silence. Multiple bangs and flashes followed, more than I could count before it got quiet again. I took Caretakers advice and resisted running toward *Slack Tide*. After five minutes of silence, I heard the sound of an ambulance and several police cars approaching, and I cautiously started walking down the dock.

Two hours later, we were sitting at *Hunks* enjoying a beverage. My hands were still shaking. Caretaker had that, "*even if I shit my pants you will never know* it" look. I knew after a few drinks he would loosen up and tell me what went down. He tried to sound as casual as possible.

"One of the DEA pukes shined his flashlight on a badge, announced who they were, and prepared to board the boat and arrest the crooks for suspicion of possession of narcotics with intent to sell. It couldn't have been two seconds later that one of them responded with a shot." He made a gun sign with his thumb and forefinger. "That's when the shit hit the fan. Before the Fed fired a single return shot, I was already on my fourth round."

Caretaker smiled grimly, "It's understandable. Most of them probably have a hundred hours on the range without ever having fired a shot in action."

"And?", I quizzed him.

"Oh, I definitely got on the scoreboard. Forty five caliber rounds at twenty feet aren't very accurate, but if you do connect, they make a mess, to say the least. I don't think that gang ever had a chance of winning that firefight, but I would guess all had records and didn't want to go back to prison."

"So one of them fired the first shot?" I asked. "What or who did they hit?"

Caretaker turned toward me and lifted his shirt. There was a bruise the size of a saucer with the colors of a baboon's ass just below his left nipple.

"Kevlar vests stop a bullet, but they don't stop the impact," he said with a grim look. "I might have a cracked rib. This was probably more than a nine-millimeter. More like a thirty-eight. But", he said with a smile, raising his glass, "It didn't break my drinking arm."

They found a couple of hundred pounds of fentanyl in the bait box, enough drugs to kill half of Miami. They managed to remove it before *Slack Tide* gently settled to the bottom of the Bight, full of bullet holes. The Coast Guard hauled it off and pulled it out so it could be used as evidence. Since everyone involved in the smuggling program is dead, there's not much chance the "evidence" will ever be used in a trial.

Jane? The DEA got a warrant and searched Jimmy's house. They didn't find any drugs, and her frail look and a story of an innocent victim of a drug dealer held up. There were no prior marks on her record. I knew I had no business connecting with her again; The cops barely signed off on my drug overdose being a complete accident. Caretaker had a different opinion of Jane and didn't mind rubbing my nose in it.

Either way, I let that relationship quietly fade away.

What Happens in Key West...

Wayne Gales

17

After a month, I figured I would never hear from Jane again. Caretaker thought differently.

As usual, he was right.

One morning, I was having breakfast at *Pepe's* with Caretaker and my phone chirped. I looked at the display and saw it was Jane's number. "Hi, Brody. I have a favor to ask. I'm going to fly out to my aunt Grace's in Cincinnati. I can't afford this townhouse anymore, and I'm going to move in with her. Could you give me a ride to the airport?"

That was an innocent enough request. Jane didn't drive, and I don't think she had a lot of money left after paying her "private eyes". I agreed to pick her up at four.

"Come along with me to say goodbye to our 'client'? I asked. Caretaker answered, while he pushed a bite of omelet under his mustache. "I think not," he said slowly, "Being as I sorta killed her husband." Looking up with a thin smile, he added, "That might be a little awkward."

He had a point there.

When I pulled up at four, I was expecting to see her waiting in front of the house, but she was nowhere in sight. I parked the Jeep and knocked on the front door. Jane answered in a bathrobe, slippers, and wet hair. "Sorry, I'm running late," she said, toweling off her hair.

"The Delta flight's not until six." Opening the door wider, she offered, "Come on in, I'll fix you a drink while I get ready. Jimmy had some booze in the cupboard." With a grim smile, she added, "I don't think he'll need it anymore. Rum and Coke okay?"

I wasn't going to mention her late husband until she did.

She did.

I stumbled over the words, "Uh, I'm sorry about Jimmy."

"I cried non-stop for two weeks," Jane said. I could imagine a little tear running down her cheek. "I knew he had a record, but I thought that activity was behind him." She dabbed a corner of her eye with the towel. "I guess I didn't see what he was up to." With a deep sigh, she added, "All I can do is move on. I'm sure you understand."

The house was dark. I flipped on the kitchen light switch. "Light bulb out?", I asked. "Oh, I've already ordered the electricity turned off", she answered while pulling down a half-gallon bottle of rum and opening a Coke. "I thought it was going to be shut off tomorrow, but the power went off an hour ago." Taking one of those metal sports cups out of the cupboard, she held it toward me. "Will this be okay? The Coke's warm, I'll add some ice." She closed the plastic lid and put a metal straw in the hole. Handing it to me, she explained, "I hope that's okay," she said, pointing at the metal straw. "I abhor paper straws, and I won't use plastic. Environment and all that, you know."

I put the straw to my lips and nodded approval. "Good", I agreed.

Turning toward the bedroom, she looked over her shoulder, "I'd love to invite you to follow me for a little snuggle, but the time's running a little tight. I hope you understand." Without answering, I waved my understanding with a hand.

A little later, Jane called out from the bedroom. "Just a few more minutes, Brody. I'll be right out."

When I didn't answer, she didn't come out of the room or ask if I heard her.

Caretaker was right.

It wasn't a few minutes but nearly a half hour. Jane emerged from the bedroom towing a full-size hardshell Samsonite suitcase, dressed in a calf-length leather skirt with a matching blazer over a lime green tank top. Her blond hair was spiked straight up, and big loop earrings bracketed her fully made-up face. Her three-inch heels made loud clicking sounds on the tile floor. She froze in her tracks when she saw me sitting in the living room on an easy chair.

Alive.

"Well, well," I said sarcastically. "It's a miracle! "Plain Jane has come out of her cocoon, and I owe Caretaker a hundred bucks." She stood motionless, looking at me and then the sports cup. "As they say, once burned, twice shy," I explained. "Someone tried that a few years ago. She didn't quite kill me but left me with all those scars on my back, a feature I'm sure you noticed, but never mentioned."

Pulling out my phone, I started to punch buttons. "Caretaker bet me that you would try this. I took him up on the bet. If he was wrong, I made a hundred bucks. If he was right, that was a cheap price to pay for living through the night, and if you succeeded, well, I wouldn't have to pay since I would be dead. Either way, it's a win-win."

Jane's eyes darted toward the garage door. I dangled a key ring around my index finger. I smiled again. "Looking for these?" I said. "I've never seen a bike lock

93

on a BMW key fob." Motioning toward the couch, I offered, "Cop a squat, Jane, if that's really your name. People will be here in a few minutes to help you get a whole new zip code, but it won't be Cincinnati."

Punching the rest of the numbers on my phone, I put it to my ear and added, "You were in this drug business up to your neck with Jimmy, and you figured out a way to get the whole gang out of the way quick and easy. You knew they wouldn't surrender, so you helped me arrange a suicide by cop." I wasn't smiling now. "And it almost worked. How tidy." I continued, "And you were going to leave me here in this house for a week or so until someone found my body. You are one cold fucking bitch."

Her first move was sudden and unexpected. Without a word, she dropped the suitcase handle, took two steps toward the kitchen table, opened the drink cup, and drained it. Yelling "Stop!" I dropped the phone and ran across the room.

Jane collapsed into my arms with a little smile.

Wayne Gales

Epilogue

The paramedics got there in seven minutes. They were just finishing a call downtown. They arrived as fast as they could, but it was too late. I could have done mouth-to-mouth, but touching lips with mine that had just swallowed a lethal dose of Fentanyl scared me. That she just tried to kill me five minutes earlier might have made me hesitate, too.

The cops found two IDs on Jane, a driver's license for Jane Jones, and a whole other one for one Audry Bangher. New Jersey driver's license, credit cards and even the Beemer SUV was registered to Audrey. She had it all figured out. Get rid of her husband, get me out of the picture, and vanish into the sunset with a whole new identity.

How'd that work for ya, Jane?

I figured the suitcase she was dragging would have clothes and drugs, but it had over a hundred grand in cash. I guess her role in this gang was turning commodities into assets.

Yes, Caretaker made me pay him the hundred dollars, a bargain considering the alternative. I couldn't let it pass with just a handshake- I handed him a bag at *Schooner Wharf* with a hundred dollars–In nickels. I did it loudly, borrowing the microphone the band was using.

Holding the bag up, I announced, "Here's to my friend Caretaker, for saving my sorry ass, a debt gratefully paid!"

He got a standing ovation. I'm glad he wasn't carrying. He would have shot me for that stunt where I stood.

I guess I need to learn how to read women a little better.

But then, my dad never did.

As for my "crime"? I was charged with a misdemeanor, received no fine, and a sentence suspended for helping them break up a drug ring. As my father said, I should have a healthy respect for the law, and try to not get caught breaking it.

Helen and the shipwreck? They submitted all the paperwork to the Bahamian government, took careful GPS readings of the location, and returned my anchor to me. A month later after a mild tropical depression had come through, the entire area was covered with three feet of sand. When the Bahamians came out with *Hoedown* to locate the site for a salvage permit, they couldn't rediscover the location.

One second of GPS measurement is a hundred and one feet. As Dad often said, it's a big ocean. Three feet of sand might as well be three hundred.

They wouldn't issue a permit for a wreck that might be there.

Oh well, easy come, easy go.

There could be as much as a billion dollars in gold, silver, emeralds, and priceless artifacts lying scattered on the bottom all over the Caribbean, Gulf of Mexico, and the Eastern coast of Florida.

Some day, some day.

Wayne Gales

Made in United States
Orlando, FL
06 June 2025

61904178R00066